Rising Flux

A Prequel Novella to Molten Flux

Jonathan Weiss

HELIXIC BOOKS

For my wife Kayla, and anyone else who has put up with my chaotic aspirations.

CONTENTS

CHAPTER ONE

BAIT

RETTIC'S BOOTS WEREN'T MADE for trekking over dunes. It was a fact he scorned himself for neglecting as he stumped his way uphill to the crest he'd been ordered to. The finely buckled and polished-leather footwear was meant to fill him with a sense of pride and status when he was to stride through the hallowed passages of the Academy of Breggesa. But all they did now was fill his feet with blisters and his gut with a vertigo as if he were about to topple over.

Two weeks of slogging through the Droughtlands with the four others of his expedition crew had only spurned the former and failed to quell the latter. Going without the accursed things on the red sands wouldn't solve the problem. The only way to make the discomfort bearable was for Rettic to constantly remind himself of their saving grace the first day they'd set out.

Barely clutched under his arm was what Rettic swore up and down was a malfunctioning prototype. It was called a Gyurian Axle, after its creator, which at least informed him who's foot to drop it on when he returned so they could see where Rettic had come up with the idea of bolting a handle to the unwieldy exterior.

According to the field medic of their party, Anora, his ill-purposed boots had protected him from laceration, even if the blow had punched a hole in the leather that leaked sand no matter how much he attempted to patch it.

Rettic limped on with a grumble. As the scribe for this expedition, he was tasked both with learning as much as he could from the crew's activities and also surveying the various environs they happened across.

'If only I could write down *only* what I saw,' Rettic muttered to himself halfway up the dune.

A sudden change in the Academy of Breggesa's tedium of a bureaucracy meant a scrawled summary of the sights wasn't good enough! No, some member of the proverbial cult Rettic thought of as "yesterday's geniuses" had designed a supposedly more precise and far more cumbersome method of research. He hefted the metal case out from under his arm and onto his shoulder, giving his aching ribs a break from the way the blasted thing's edges bit into his chest.

Finally at the dune's peak, Rettic let the fragile instrument's case fall unceremoniously into the sand. But he'd only created more work for himself. With a sigh, Rettic lowered himself to his knees and began digging out the heavy case, now half-buried from the impact just to spite him.

While the exterior of the case had been infuriatingly uniform, the interior was the opposite. It was a mess of gears, sliding rails with spring-loaded wires, delicate rods of iron that hooked into unseen latches to connect one lever to another, all centred around the gimbal-mounted golden Axle that had —once again— fallen out of position.

'I don't know why I expected anything else,' Rettic said to himself as he reached in to fix it. One more suggestion he'd make to the contraption's designer was a touch more room to work among the machinery, if only for the mercy of his scabbed and raw cuticles. The gyro slotted into place with a sharp *click*, a motion he'd learnt to quickly whip his hands away from to avoid his fingers being pinched among its workings. Anora may have cauterised the bleeding, yet she couldn't mend his pride. On leaving Breggesa, he'd been sure he was the brightest of his class, yet the machine's constant rebellion made him wonder if he'd learnt anything at all.

Now in place, it was supposed to spin. Rettic gave the side of the case an open-palmed slap, but the gimbal defied it. With a reluctant sigh, he reached back into the workings, giving no caution to his fingers as they wormed into every cavity to find another dozen loose components.

It was only then he realised that in his frustration he'd completely forgotten to take in the view. He chuckled to himself. Probably why they introduced the Gyurian Axle in the first place.

The cluster of towers stood a mile or more to the south, ensconced by rolling blankets of dunes. They bore hides of hyper-machined steel and impossibly smooth glass, stretching to heights that would dwarf the grandest buildings back at Breggesa. They were arranged in a circle, a spiked perimeter to silently ward off trespassers, not from walking among them, but from delving into the unfathomable depths hidden below.

Decades of study represented their attempts to glean more of the ruins' creators, but they could still only refer to them as "those-of-glass." Their expedition leader, Archarus, had previously made the journey to this particular cluster of dormant spires, yet he'd so far refused to share even a hint of what had come of the failed expedition.

"A fresh mind is more open for learning than an expectant one."

He'd stubbornly repeated this mantra each time a member of the current expedition inquired into the tale of his last visit.

When Rettic was the last of their number without the sense to stop asking, he'd been rebuffed with a phrase far sterner.

This had only done more to spur his imagination, mixing the rambling tales of ancient Academy scholars into his own wild assumptions. The magic they studied and utilised was bound and logical, a language born out of blocky runes painted onto skin, their colour and effects dependent on which blood one hailed from.

The beady green eyes he'd inherited from his parents marked him as a Kretatic. His magic allowed him to harness the magnetism innately contained within hunks of scrap metal to assemble them into controllable machines called arcanites.

Rettic glanced down at the three runes on his arm, their green hue flashing in the sunset's light. He'd prepared them at the bottom of the hill in anticipation of use with the Gyurian Axle, but it was more tempting to use them to possess the metal itself to figure out why the damn thing wasn't working. But that would require two more runes.

'Not for waste,' Rettic chided to himself. 'I've fixed you before without an axiom and I'll fix you again.'

Each rune corresponded to a word, an instruction, and together that series of instructions was an axiom, statements of change for the world around them dependent on their order, intention and, most importantly, ink.

The rare liquid was concocted from the water sealed into the air itself, an impossible feat accomplished by a people unlike his, who could conjure storms over the barren lands. Supposedly. They were long dead now, extinct to the point any story of them was a gassed-up legend. When he was first told about it, it was along with the word "ocean," supposedly a body of enough liquid water to cover the entire Droughtlands.

The thought was dismissed as a wild fantasy. Another *click* sounded within the case and Rettic whipped his hands out, scratching the back of his left on a sharpened rail despite himself. Nevertheless, the Axle began to spin lazily, and he allowed himself a sigh of relief. He took another moment of respite to survey the ruins again, their mystery still obscured to him in a haze of frustration and exhaustion. From this far away, the instruments were unlikely to pick up even a hint of something abnormal. Rettic reluctantly looked back at his left wrist.

With little more than a thought, the emerald green runes began sliding to the centre of his palm, each one burning white and hot before the next stacked atop it to do the same. When the third was done, Rettic motioned his hand over the Axle and unleashed the axiom, savouring the crackling thrill of his influence sweeping through the contraption's workings.

Every screw, rivet and spring was suddenly his, a twisting and contorted network of clanking guts that rumbled hungrily with his own. The Axle spun in his mind, faster and faster as the physical counterpart's tip slowly revolved in a circle.

It revolved as he'd anticipated, spare for hesitating

momentarily to point back towards the encampment. The reading was expected, after all. It was rumoured the runes and axioms they employed were descended from those-of-glass, a form of magic the Axle was supposedly designed to pick up.

Today it halted a second time.

Rettic forced his eyes to focus —a difficult task from how much of his consciousness had to be dedicated to the machine— and slowly realised it was pointing towards the ruins. He should've expected it, but the astonishment was still too much of a spanner-in-the-works for his mind to keep hold of the arcanite. The contraption's innards suddenly screeched and groaned, and Rettic couldn't help but doing the same.

Rettic set about repairing the Axle for the umpteenth time. Out of the corner of his eye he could vaguely make out what he thought was the bulky form of Hanwark, the self-proclaimed muscle of the expedition. His suspicion was confirmed by the slurring drawl that followed.

'You said this is your first trip out of the Academy, right?' Hanwark said as he stumped up the dune.

Rettic cursed himself. The oaf already knew the answer to the question because he'd asked it nearly a dozen times before. He shouldn't have admitted it all those weeks ago when he'd first met the rest of this crew. On the other hand, the constantly breaking instrument would have given him away as a novice eventually, no matter how much he blamed its shoddy workmanship.

Hanwark continued without prompting, taking a knee next to Rettic so heavily that the dune under him threatened to slip. 'No one said you looked too damn young for it?'

'Twenty is of age,' Rettic replied as tersely as possible. At least this question was new.

'Might be,' Hanwark mused. 'But not for this line of work.'

'Twenty is of age,' Rettic repeated. 'If it's good enough for the Academy—'

He was cut off with a chuckle and a flapping wave, and he wasn't sure which made him fume the most.

'State of the Academy, anyone's good enough for them! Desperate doesn't make for a good standard, something you should remember.'

'But I'm not desperate!'

'Never said you was,' Hanwark said, putting up his hands in a mock surrender. 'Academy's been taking on dead weights for years, anyway, so no need to hide it if you are. But that's been their problem, see?'

Rettic shook his head and turned back to his instruments, exaggerating the motions of untangling its guts on the off chance Hanwark would take the hint and leave him alone.

'It's these places, boy—'

'Don't call me boy,' Rettic snapped.

'—For how much mystery that's hidden within, it's a puzzle, and everyone they send to solve it needs to know as much as they can to get it right and get out with something useful.'

'Like a paralict,' Rettic stated. Something snapped deep within the case and gave a tinny tinkle, a sound Hanwark mercifully didn't notice.

'Like their lives.'

Rettic looked at him. The half-toothed grin he'd become sick of smelling was now stony and hollow.

'Not a threat,' Hanwark said quietly. 'Just a warning. Just want you to think about what you do here. Why you're here.'

With great difficulty, Rettic suppressed a scoff before answering. 'I'm a scribe, am I not? I'm here to help out where needed, of course, but I understand my main purpose is to be one of learning for future expeditions.'

'And you don't think me and the others can do just that?'

'Well— I didn't mean that—'

'It was rhetorical,' Hanwark chuckled out. 'Rett-or-ic-al! Geddit?'

'I wish I didn't,' he grumbled. 'Is that what this "counselling" of yours is for?'

Hanwark shook his head, leaning closer despite the camp sitting two hundred paces back down the dune. 'What's Archarus doing, right now, I mean?'

It felt like he was being led on, but Rettic looked back down the slope for what little he could make out. Archarus, the expedition's chief, was exactly where he'd been an hour ago when he'd tasked Rettic with surveying the ruin site, cross-legged and in the shade of his tent, scribbling away in that ragged journal of his.

'Writing a report,' Rettic eventually brought himself to answer.

'Seems like a job for a scribe, right?' Hanwark snapped back.

'But he tasked me to—'

'Play with that little metal box? He's a metal mouth—'

'Don't call us that!' Rettic spat, for all the good it would do.

'—just like you, so why doesn't he do it? Probably would be less likely to break the damn thing the way you just did. Anyway, I ain't ever heard of an expedition taking more than one Kretatic!'

Rettic swore again, and it elicited another infuriating chuckle from the brute before they continued.

'Anora might be a Curiktic like me, but she's a damn sight sharper than I ever was, much as I hate to say it. Just a few axioms and she'll see anything your little box has missed. Then Pelstow's our scout, because no expedition is going ahead without a Reythurist. Sky's too valuable to leave empty of a set of eyes, isn't it?'

'I'm very aware,' Rettic muttered. While the arcanite creations he or Archarus could spur into life may afford their kin flexibility of how they applied their abilities, their options were quite literally weighed down by the metal's unavoidable property of being so damn heavy.

'So then the question I don't want to ask —but one you damn sure better be asking yourself— is what's the Academy getting from sending a bright-eyes like you out to tag along with old and seasoned hands like us?'

There was a genuine look in Hanwark's eyes that made Rettic's mouth flap as he tried to answer. It only lasted a second, but it was enough to give the brute the rare satisfaction of having made a good point.

'I'm here for learning,' Rettic said as he slammed the instrument case shut. He got to his feet, grappling the Axle back onto his shoulder.

Hanwark rose as well, his knees creaking like pressured iron. 'Yeah, learning. The thing the Academy is so damn desperate to say they're all about. But are you to learn from what happens to us, or are we to learn from what happens to you?' He turned away from the view of the ruins and started plodding back to the camp. 'It ain't a threat, remember that! Just... just keep it in mind.'

Yet Rettic couldn't understand how his last words could be anything *but* a threat. A flood of worry washed his stomach as cursed words his father had sworn him to never say flowed as a running stream.

How had he not seen it? He'd prided himself on his methods of observation. It was what he was sure got him accepted into the Academy in the first place. Why, it was even the reason he told himself he'd earned the quickly fading privilege of the fifth spot of this expedition! All this time he'd ignored the fact that he'd never met another person in the Academy that wasn't either his age or more than double it.

He wasn't a student.

He was bait.

CHAPTER TWO

APPROACH

THERE WAS LITTLE DIFFERENCE between the bedrolls provided by the Academy's commissary and the fine sand furnished by the lands of their journey. They provided an uncomfortable night's sleep that made Rettic miss the comforts of his own quarters. Subterranean rooms dotted the Academy's campus, cool and immune to the sun's whims, something the patchwork animal hides of their cramped two-to-a-tent lodgings couldn't mimic.

Many things kept him awake that night. Pelstow's shrill snores came from the other end of the tent, accompanied by his ever-twitching legs. The stiffness in Rettic's hips from trudging up and down loose dunes for weeks. The prospect of being among the haunting walls of a ruin for the first time.

But Hanwark just *had* to go and add a few more items to that list. Every other thought he'd had thus far on the journey seemed petulant compared to what the brute had raised. Rettic played the conversation again and again in his mind, trying to figure out the right words he could have interjected with to justify his membership on this expedition.

But nothing came.

Rettic's worry grew.

He'd spent his formative years dismissing the tales of indescribable phenomena hidden away in the ruins and the horrors they wrought. It was his main driver to join the damn Academy in the first place, to explain away what terrified him the most. But now he was about to stumble blindly into one as a precaution to save more valuable minds.

Rettic tried to shift to a more comfortable position, his tossing and turning only threatening to tip over the walls of the tent. If this were to be his final days, he thought darkly, at least he wouldn't have to put up with more nights in such cramped confines. How the others had been doing this for decades was beyond him. Archarus was the oldest of their five, so well-seasoned he'd likely been pelted with offers for cushy posts that involved residence in sprawling manors and little more effort than pouring over the kinds of reports he'd spent his life creating.

For him to come back to this same ruin was astounding. The superstitious scholars of the Academy of Breggesa —which made up most of them— refused to travel to the same ruins twice for what may be awaiting them.

Whatever lay within the debris left by those-of-glass must have been too captivating to be forgotten, yet that was no reason for their leader to keep it a mystery. Then again, he was a mystery himself.

The moment Rettic had received his invitation for the journey he'd dashed through the sprawling nightmare of the Academy of Breggesa's archives and its many rows of once-ordered report files to pick out any hint of Archarus' past, only to find someone had beaten him to it. For the first time, the archives were lacking.

In contrast to his scurrying worries, the rest of the crew seemed more than content to leave their leader's past as unknown. Rettic continued inventing stories until sunrise, finally dozing off just as Pelstow twitched a touch too violently.

'My apologies, Rettic,' he yawned. 'Don't know about you, but I could barely sleep.'

'You too?'

Pelstow sat up and pushed his long sandy hair back into a rough tail, fixing it in place with a leather loop as he ground his jaw back into place. 'Air around here smells funny.'

'Oh,' Rettic said involuntarily as the other man cracked a sly grin. It was a tired gag he'd doggedly repeated every morning, to the point Rettic could only fume at himself for being caught in it again. Of course they all smelt awful, they hadn't seen a clean rag for days!

Pelstow added insult to injury by adding his trademark blue-eyed wink to the mix, as if to impress upon a child that it was he and his people that were marked with the axioms to manipulate air.

As they ate that morning, Rettic had to stop himself from glancing at their leader too often, but it looked as though he'd suffered a similar night of malcontent. He usually made the effort to twist his weathered cheeks into a soft grin, to give the appearance of a benevolent mentor, yet today his expression was blank, his green-eyed stare fixed on something that lay far beyond the bounds of their camp.

It continued as they hauled on their packs and began the day's trek. When he snuck a glimpse across his shoulder, he'd only seen more sand dunes as the subject of Archarus' stare. Only once they were walking did he realise what was beyond them. The group crested the dune Rettic had visited the previous night, pausing for a moment to take in the view. He looked over to Archarus. His face remained expressionless as he scanned the horizon.

'Last night's Axle?' Archarus eventually said with a calm

voice.

'Two stops,' Rettic stammered back. He cursed himself for not keeping his tone level before he continued. 'A small one for us, as expected, then one for what lies ahead. Completely stilled for it.'

'What's it meant to detect again?' Anora asked from a few steps behind them. She was stubbier woman than most, her short legs the only thing holding Rettic back from complaining aloud about the slog until she'd done so first, but she was far too spritely to give him the chance. Similar to Hanwark, it was a question asked many times before, not out of mocking but instead out of fear of replacement.

Her yellow eyes also marked her a Curiktic, with axioms to access anything the sun provided in nearly any form she saw fit. Fire, light, warmth, it was all there, and when used in concert could detect even the slightest anomaly in the environment. The exact thing the Gyurian Axle was invented to do while using far less precious ink.

'Anomalies and fractures in the land,' Rettic said patiently. Maybe she'd forgotten or couldn't wrap her head around it. He barely could himself. She was the kindest among them, the least he could do was give her the benefit of the doubt.

However, Pelstow wasn't nearly as charitable.

'You're telling me that box you keep hissing under your breath about can tell us *that*—' he pointed dramatically at the ruins, '—is going to have something weird in it!?'

Hanwark guffawed as Rettic stewed silently. It made no sense to pick fun at him for having to use the damn thing. Why not Archarus for always ordering him to do so, or even the Academy for saddling him with it in the first place?

It always felt a low blow to be mocked for simply doing as he was told.

'Take a look for us Pelstow,' Archarus said. 'Keep high and meet us at the outskirts.'

'Do I need to take that box with me? Might weigh me down!'

More howls of laughter erupted from Hanwark and Rettic felt his guts boil. Pelstow took a knee, withdrawing from a satchel under his cloak a paint brush and a small glass vial half-full of sky-blue ink. He held the brush in his teeth as he unstoppered it, likely the only action he ever took care with, then set to work etching four runes into his left wrist. The ink dried as a tattoo the moment it touched his skin, its colour flowing to the square corners of each rune as if they were stencilled. When he was done, Pelstow stowed his equipment and slid the axiom into his palm.

The rest of the party had only a second to brace themselves before a blast of dust rocketed outwards from Pelstow's feet. Hacking out a lungful of sand, Rettic found himself wishing he had the face of a munbrak. As ugly as those delicious beasts of burden may be, their scaled nostrils could clamp shut at a moment's notice and stay that way for hours.

The remaining four resumed their trek towards the ruins,

the undulating sands quickly engulfing the horizon. It left Rettic with a slight tinge of envy not to be born a Reythurist. It would've meant less walking, but maybe it wasn't worth being as insufferable as Pelstow.

The soaring Reythurist returned to their company an hour later, touching down with another barrage of sand that caught Rettic off-guard.

'Do you need to come in so close?' Anora said almost pleadingly.

'By your footsteps you've already shown a safe landing. Would you rather I risk new ground up ahead?'

She and Rettic shared a look, deciding not to rise to the goad. Not while this close to the ruins. A hundred more paces and he'd be able to touch the enormous glass walls of the nearest tower. To press his brow close and peer in, searching for ancient secrets.

He drew a breath as he stared at the most promising window, tempering his expectations. In a structure so large, not every room or cavity could contain something worth study. It was more likely to house something that would kill them.

'Your report?' Archarus asked Pelstow. 'I saw you skim lower than I'd like.'

'Then we have differing notions of what is high.'

'No lower than the tallest point of the ruins,' Archarus said.

'Ah.' Pelstow blushed as he glanced back to the ruin, his eyes tracing across the midriff of the exposed portion of the towers.

'Just over two dozen in total. No grid pattern, circular layout, if anything. Nothing in the middle of it, either. Might make for a good camp, but I'd watch out for the westmost tower. It looks fallen towards the centre but I can't see a fault on its length and it leans heavily into another.'

'What could that mean?' Rettic asked.

'Means it ain't broken, but it ain't built like that,' Hanwark answered. 'So it's the third thing.'

'A fracture of some kind?'

Anora and Hanwark flinched, the pair already more superstitious than the rest of the crew.

'Sorry,' Rettic added.

'We'll make for the centre,' Archarus said. 'We can begin readings from there.' He glanced up at the midday sun overhead. 'Stay out of the shadows. Easy for now, but... just remember it anyway.'

He led the approach, the other three in convoy behind him and Rettic bringing up the rear with the cumbersome Axle. If Archarus had been here before, surely he knew it would be safe, right? The course he set was confident, directly between the first two towers then under the bridge formed between the next set. At least the dunes were low here, if not completely flat, affording him the opportunity to gawp up at the scene.

The smooth plates of glass that walled the towers were set in curving panes far larger than any living soul had the wits to attempt creating. The darkness beyond was hidden by the reflection they bore of wobbling blue sky and orange sand. It was only interrupted by banded columns of steel, or on the rare and more enticing occasion, a shattered portion high up that exposed the structure's guts to the elements.

But they weren't a point of entry.

This was one of the fractures Rettic had studied so vehemently. The glass was shattered, yes, but the resultant shards still hung in the air, a motionless orbit around a small, black ball the size of Rettic's clenched fist. He counted under his breath as he watched it, registering a slight quiver in its position every three or four seconds.

Thankfully, none of these fractures had appeared at ground level and once they'd reached the centre clearing, Rettic felt safe enough to breath a touch easier. Pelstow may have teased him the whole trip about the "funny air that supposedly surrounded him," but now the joke made Rettic imagine a far more dangerous reality.

'We'll make camp here?' Anora asked, hurling her pack at her feet.

Hanwark let out something between a bark and a yelp before he figured out he had intelligible words at his disposal. 'We'll be in shadow in an hour if we camp in that spot. We're still avoiding shadow, right?'

Archarus nodded and Hanwark continued.

'Fifty paces that-a-way will keep us in sun. No idea how you feel about night, Archarus, but that's what we have to work with.'

Rettic squinted to the unremarkable patch of ground indicated, only cottoning on once Hanwark was trudging over to it what was so special about it. For the almost arbitrary alignment of the ranks of towers, the pair of rings gave way to exactly two gaps that allowed a view back out into the desert, east and west, to afford them full exposure to the rising and setting sun.

Once he'd deposited his pack and the Gyurian Axle within the boundary Hanwark had drawn in the sand with a dragging foot, he doubled back to try help Anora with her own back, not that she'd let him.

'Rettic!' Archarus called. 'The Axle, take a scan.'

'But it's not sunset,' he said stupidly. 'Bit strange, isn't it?'

'Many things are strange here.'

'That something you reckon or that you know?' Pelstow asked as he pitched his and Rettic's tent.

Archarus ignored the jibe with a patience Rettic could only dream off as he joined him on his right in front of the Axle, taking a knee as Rettic began to put the fallen components back into place.

'In my day I tried inventing something like this,' he said quietly.

Something clattered under Rettic's left thumb and he struggled to find it again. It was the first time the whole journey Archarus had spoken to him alone.

'I wish you had,' he stammered back in response. 'Hopefully would have done a better job at it, too.'

Archarus grinned, properly this time. 'If I had, it's what I would be using right now.'

Rettic hesitated for a moment but thought nothing of it. It was Hanwark's words getting in his head again.

'But, we all need to find a reason to not to be forgotten somehow. I'll find mine soon. One day you'll find yours.'

'How soon?' Rettic said slowly.

The grin briefly turned to a chuckle. 'Don't let that worry you, Rettic. And don't let the others give you a hard time. These types of expeditions need the banter. Keeps you from thinking of other things.'

He glanced up at Archarus. The grin was still there, still with a life that Rettic hadn't seen before today, yet his dull green eyes didn't share it. There was a question in the air, just hanging on a hook like bait.

Like him.

He didn't bite.

He instead withdrew his ink and brush from his satchel, a task made difficult by his shaking hands. The three runes took a little longer to form on his skin than usual, a sluggishness Rettic put down to the pressure of his silent mentor watching over his every move. He forced the axiom to his palm, waving his hand over the mechanics and commandeering them to life.

But it didn't feel like the last dozen times. More control

flowed outwards through the case, tendrils of it like stinging roots snaking down into the earth beyond the metal itself.

His heart pounded as he tried to hold his focus, brushing aside the thought of a bolt or wire he'd not repaired properly. But worse took its place. His governing touch was suddenly rocketing uncontrollably into the earth, ricocheting through the lattice of frames buried deep below the towers, past ore deposits and then beyond that —most terrifying of all— nothing.

A hand clapped on his shoulder, a blow so puny compared to the colossus his skin felt like as his senses burrowed onwards, yet just enough to snap him out of it. Archarus was back at his side, his eyes now fixed on the gimbal as it began to spin. Rettic felt like his head was doing same and it took almost all his willpower to stay upright without filling the case with his breakfast.

The golden tip turned in an achingly gradual arc, spinning counter clockwise until it reached Archarus, where the needle stopped dead. Rettic relinquished control of the machine as the gimbal's momentum tore it from its socket, wreaking havoc on the rest of the contraption.

'That's... that's...'

Rettic's foggy mind lost all sense of words as he turned to Archarus. The grin was gone. His eyes were hollow.

'Strange?' he said quietly. 'Many things are strange here. Best not to think about it.'

He tried stammering again, still trying to make sense of what the Axle had done, but Archarus had already left his side, walking alone towards the ruined towers. Rettic looked back to the case, dreading the extent of repairs it demanded.

Despite slipping from its holding and even the damage done to the mechanical guts, the needle still hovered and spun in place over the mess of wires and sprockets, its tip resolutely tracking Archarus' path.

CHAPTER THREE

WARNING

RETTIC SLAMMED THE CASE shut. Part of him wanted to just bury the damn thing in the sand. What if it had been malfunctioning the entire journey and he'd been a fool having faith in it? But as he stared at the dull and dented metal shell of the device, he knew he could not comfort himself with a lie.

The metal never lies.

It was an old Kretatic saying. What you felt, it felt, and doubting it was a sure-fire way of losing control, either of the arcanite or of your own mind. The skin on the back of his neck prickled at the last idea, intensified by the scorching midday sun. If Archarus hadn't slapped his shoulder when he had, he would've been lost to the machine.

Rettic had never found the bounds of his control to be so chaotic. There'd been times when simple hunks of scrap and ore momentarily broke his focus, this time it was the absence of it that had shaken him.

'I'm not meant to find nothing,' Rettic whispered to himself as he hefted the case into his arms. Maybe he should just bury the thing, and let some other poor sod dig it up in a few thousand years' time. Rettic let out a much-needed chuckle.

'Something funny?' Pelstow called over from the camp.

Rettic's brain froze as he begged it for a single note of snark or wit to respond with, yet when nothing came, he resigned himself to silently stumping over to the tents and dropping the Axle into the sand near one of the tent flaps.

'Still don't understand the point of that thing,' Pelstow said.

This drew a disapproving glare from Anora, sitting a few feet away.

'It detects fractures without triggering or disturbing them,' Rettic said mechanically.

'And how do you know that?' he teased.

'Do you actually have any interest in the answer?' Anora snapped.

Pelstow's grin faulted, returning a touch more hollow when

he next spoke. 'Our purpose at the Academy is to learn, is it not? I'd gamble from how much you've been fuming about your little contraption that what you just said is what they told you, and you're just going along with it, right?'

Rettic frowned as he lowered himself down to the sand. The question was all too similar to what Hanwark had asked yesterday.

'I've got no choice aside from believing them. You haven't let me forget it's my first expedition, so what else should I do but what I am told?'

'Best not to think about it,' Anora said quickly, still glaring at Pelstow.

'I think we should.' Pelstow's voice lowered as he leaned in, glancing at the distant forms of Archarus and Hanwark before continuing. The pair stalked among the rings of towers with paths dictated by the shadowy borders they threw. 'Archarus has been here before and what you just said is *exactly* what he's been telling us the entire time. But we don't know what he found, who he was with, or if they even made it back. What if something went wrong with the attempt and he's about to risk *our* damn necks to try again?'

'That's why you flew low,' Rettic said. 'To find the last party.'

'And I found nothing. Makes me all the more scared, I tell you. So I don't know if your Axle is just a boondoggle or if it actually finds things, but you need to tell us if Archarus is hiding anything.'

Before he could respond with a pre-prepared lie, Rettic's throat closed up. He glanced at the case, his paranoia screaming at him that the needle was still bouncing around in there, straining to make its accusation. He looked back to Pelstow who'd raised an eyebrow. Could he tell him? Did he even know how to explain what he'd felt?

'It just picked up the regular fractures.' Rettic said too late. 'Nothing more.'

'Tell me when you find something, then,' Pelstow leaned back, a cool breath escaping his lips. 'You've been awfully quiet, Anora.'

She nodded.

'Something you don't want to think about?'

'You damn well know what that is.'

Anora didn't need to explain further. Rettic already knew. A shadow dancer. A person turned into a walking fracture, guardian of those-of-glass and maddener of all they encounter. Was that why the Axle pointed to Archarus?

They didn't share another word on the matter. The shadows of the ruins stretched deeper by the hour and thankfully Hanwark's cautioning had been correct. Only weeks ago, Rettic would have thought it silly to avoid a simple lack of light, but the dark patches that slowly caged them into the clearing felt like an achingly slow trap being sprung.

It seemed to drain the sand of its very colour, the border between light and dark not a solid line but an ebbing haze that toyed with his nerves until he was fighting against the urge to go sprinting down the last narrowing alley of the sun's touch so as not to spend the night in this haunting spike field.

Archarus returned soon after, seemingly beyond heeding Hanwark's warning but somehow unaffected by it. Rettic watched as he stepped back over the border of light, the shape of his own figure cast on the sand a moment too late to be natural. He glanced to the others, yet none looked to have seen it.

'Everything alright?' Archarus asked him. 'Something troubling you?'

'Axle's broken,' Rettic said quickly. 'I'll try, but I'm not certain I can fix it.'

Archarus only nodded before he went to check on the others. Rettic watched him go, waiting until he was busy with an argument of spirited jargon with Anora and Hanwark before turning to the metal case.

He'd not thought of it until he'd summoned the lie, but maybe the Axle would be worth something after all. Just to check it had really pointed to Archarus. As the sun disappeared, the desert should've come alive with the calls and chirps of all manner of insects and skinks emerging from their daily graves, yet the ruins were silent. Even Pelstow's snores were absent. Rettic didn't join him. He tinkered later into the night, Anora coming to his aid as she wearily conjured a glowing orb the size of his fist.

'Careful what you find there,' she said as she placed it in the sand next to the Axle.

'I'm more worried about what I don't find.'

'I just hope we don't find it,' she slowly whispered before leaving for her tent.

Maybe she was right.

But Rettic needed certainty. In the early morning, the delicate gimbal finally snapped back into place. He paused and allowed himself a quiet yawn before retrieving a vial of ink and a brush from his satchel. The fading light of the orb barely helped as he drew the runes for control of the Gyurian Axle. Not that it was necessary. When he'd first been taught the runes, he'd burned them into his eyes for the amount of time spent staring at the page.

As the last one dried, he hesitated, the brush hovering over his arm. His understanding of this axiom was to make the device find all instances of magic, fracture or otherwise. What if he could make it find *only* the strongest?

Two more runes went onto his arm and he forced them into his palm, waving his left hand over the case as he plunged his right into the sand. It helped to have something to hold onto, something to ground himself.

The needle jolted to life, twisting rapidly to point straight down. Rettic had expected as much and pushed the reach of his control further into the ground, cautiously feeling out the skeletons of the towers below the sand like they were guide rails. The mineral deposits appeared again, tingling in his mind with their strange shapes and sharp corners, but he ignored them, pushing further until he found the void again.

The cavern felt larger than the ruins. Rettic blindly probed for a way through its ceiling, each of his gasping breaths echoing in his ears as he gripped the sand just to keep his own body present in his consciousness. A pathway presented itself, a frame of metal running around the hollow and Rettic followed it deeper, only caressing his control against it occasionally to keep his.

Soon his trembling body felt like a distant dream as his senses reached under the void.

His suspicion was right.

There *was* something down here.

The sensation flickered between walls of solid metal and vacant rock, but more was calling out for him. Rettic pushed further, passing through metal and finding so much more than steel and iron. A pulse raced in his fingertips that was not his own, the kind like when a Kretatic's resonance clashes with another.

A Kretatic's magnetic resonance was their signature, a scent that marked their territory. It flowed through every chunk of metal they controlled, even lingering in pieces they'd long forgotten. Each one was unique and this one was no exception.

It was old.

Old and tired.

The sensation sapped into Rettic. His mind slowed, his

vision dimming as he tried to blink sense back into his thoughts without losing control. He looked down and his hands had turned to silver, his grip on the sand no longer his own as he battled to retreat from the ground.

Another resonance had caught him.

A resonance that spoke in his head.

You control machines.

Rettic's mind was wrenched back into the ground and his body collapsed, his very bones now replaced by a set that felt impossibly giant as the rumbling voice spoke again.

This machine will control life.

Thousands of resonances suddenly cried out to him, each a ceaseless energy identical to the next that made his heart race before the exhaustion of the first resonance cut through and vanquished them all. It relinquished him and he desperately raced his mind back into his drained body, the voice following him one last time.

Do not control it.

Rettic slumped back into his body, the words ringing in his head. He was only aware of the sand pressed into his face as unconsciousness took him, the old and tired resonance lingering in his blood.

Hours later, he found himself face down in the sand, a forceful grip shaking him awake.

'Were your repairs successful?'

It was Archarus' voice. Crouched over him, he rolled Rettic

over and pulled him into a sitting position, an unusual concern in his dull green eyes. 'Were you successful?'

It took a few seconds to hear the repeated words over the stinging pain of his face. He touched it gingerly, cringing as he accidentally rubbed sand into the tiny gashes on his cheek. At least that was something Anora could easily fix.

Behind him, the Axle's guts were scattered around the case, a puzzle to now never be solved. Groggily, he turned back to Archarus, his whole-body swaying as he went. His mentor was still looking expectantly at him, Anora and Pelstow standing a few paces beyond.

'No... no luck. I'm sorry.'

Archarus shook his head. 'No apologies needed. We control the things we're able to and that machine looks like it was never meant to be one of them.'

'That's a shame,' Pelstow said. He glanced to Rettic with a dark, knowing look as Archarus stood up and waved for Pelstow to follow.

'We'll just have to rely on our senses, won't we?' Archarus said. 'Come on, I want to find a way into one of these structures.'

This left Rettic with Anora, who reluctantly busied herself with the scratches on Rettic's cheek.

'They're minor, not enough for me to waste ink on mending.' She drew a hollow breath. 'But I worry about what you appear to have wasted ink on.'

'You said last night you didn't want to think about it.'

'I didn't want to, but I have to. You found something, didn't you? Why else would you break your machine?'

Rettic glanced around. Archarus and Pelstow were still heading towards the wall of ruins, the latter catching his eye with a surreptitious look back. Hanwark seemed to be still asleep in his tent.

'There's something down there,' Rettic whispered. 'It spoke to me.'

Anora gasped in horror as she withdrew from him.

'Not a shadow dancer,' Rettic added quickly. 'It was in the metal. A Kretatic trick, almost like it was a person.'

'Something's *living* down there?'

'I don't know,' he said. 'It spoke of machines. I felt them. Thousands of them. All identical.'

'For this kind of thing we'd have to ask Archarus, he's the only other—'

'No,' Rettic said impulsively.

Anora's frown sagged into worry and then outright panic.

'I will figure it out,' Rettic assured her. 'There are things I need to understand before I could tell him.'

'You find them out then,' she hissed back. 'But you keep me out of it as best you can because I ain't going down there if there's something living. Only means that we'd come back dead!'

She briskly left his side, busying herself checking and

rechecking their provisions and looking adamantly at anything but him. Was he right to tell Anora? Should he have lied to her instead? What if what he'd felt wasn't even real? A sleep-deprived fever dream driven by fear and uncertainty?

But the memory of the voice was crystal clear. It had been a low, ancient rumbling that struck at his core. Like it belonged to something far older than he could ever imagine. It was as if they knew what he was when they sent their warning. But what were the thousands of other chittering forces he'd sensed with it?

These were questions he couldn't answer alone.

Questions that he could only find answers to deep underground.

Questions Archarus might already know the answer to.

CHAPTER FOUR

GLASS

H E MADE ANOTHER TOKEN attempt at repairing the Gyurian Axle, but promptly gave up when Hanwark emerged from his tent and roared with laughter at the shattered machine. Instead, he stashed whatever precious parts were yet to be buried in his satchel and left the rest behind to be consumed by the dunes.

Not wanting to be the victim of more of Hanwark's ominous warnings, he made his way over to Archarus and Pelstow, weaving a path between the ruins' patchwork of shadows. Their glass walls let the early sunlight bleed through and he had to debate with himself how dark the ground needed to be to warrant avoiding it.

There wasn't much he could do but observe as Archarus and Pelstow moved from pane to pane, touching and testing each panel of glass with surgical precision.

Academy manuals on the subject of penetrating the ruins of those-of-glass were rare, not for lack of publication or insatiable demand, but for how few scholars returned from these places, and the fewer still who thought it worthwhile to write it down so others may follow in their paths.

Fortunately for budding intellectuals of the Droughtlands, Rettic still counted himself among the latter, and with pencil and parchment he followed the pair unblinkingly. He'd expected complex instruments similar to the one he'd hefted for the past few weeks to be employed, or even freshly developed axioms yet to be shared with the word. Yet the means of testing on display were so primitive that Rettic gave up scribbling after only a few minutes.

First a handful of sand would be thrown, then pebbles, harder and closer until they were hurling the rocks from only a step away. Only when they'd run out of large enough stones did they move in to risk their own skin, reaching out with well-scarred fingers. Their touches only lasted a fraction of a second and were quickly followed by a dancing retreat.

The glass in question answered their presence by flashing dark, reflecting their own faces in a twisted vision for only a moment before fading back to translucency.

Another surprised them when it glowed brighter in the sun, blinding the three of them for a few nervous minutes. The next they tried produced what looked like a spark of energy that made Pelstow yelp and fall backwards into the sand. Rettic risked a few steps closer to observe what lay beyond the glass, spotting a small red disc of clay or some other ceramic that rolled steadily along the window's borders. He made a note of it, hoping that whoever was stuck transcribing his journals could make sense of the phrase "*red disc through window, shocking reaction.*"

It seemed an exercise of gut instinct, which explained why there was so little written on the subject. Even the most mundane potential breach points were dismissed with a silent shake of the head before they moved onto the next, no matter how banal the reaction to their presence was.

They were still going at it by late morning, the other expedition members cycling through Pelstow's place until an exasperated Hanwark was hurling not just pebbles but full-sized boulders at the glass. Rettic forced himself to watch the entire time. Not the glass, but Archarus, and he sensed the man knew this.

'Oh come on!' Hanwark roared as a stretch of glass simply consumed a handful of thrown sand with no sight of it on the other side. 'This is the fifth tower! How many days are we going to waste on this?'

'As many as it takes,' Archarus replied calmly.

'Which isn't what we have! Every second here is a risk, a week off of our lives! You've been here before, there has to be a better way to find what you're looking for.'

'With the Gyurian Axle broken we must do things the old-fashioned way, something I thought you were more than used to,' Archarus said coldly.

'But it wouldn't have found a way in,' Rettic said defensively. 'The Axle only pointed out fractures.'

'Then it would have pointed out what to avoid,' he retorted.

Their eyes met and Rettic couldn't suppress the fear in his own.

'I apologise,' Archarus said calmly. 'I forgot myself. Perhaps you're right, Hanwark. Let's take a break. I suspect we'll have better luck come the afternoon on the other side of the ruins.'

Rettic lingered near the glass as the other two began making their way back to camp. What if it was trying to keep them out? Not to protect itself, but to protect them from what lay within? From what Archarus would find? He watched their leader's back as he and Hanwark trudged away, more questions spawning in his head. What if the voice from last night had something to do with the last expedition?

The five of them talked brusquely as they ate their midday rations, the conversation firmly focused on finding the way into the ruins, despite the questions of what would come next bubbling in all their minds. It was something only Archarus seemed to know, but by the time they were all walking over to the tilted structure he'd indicated earlier, none of them had drawn up the courage to interrogate him on the matter.

Archarus' path took them into the shadows between the ruins, circling the ring until they were standing before the slanted tower. Waves of dunes lapped at its glass sides like a snake consuming its prey, drifts running into open breaches that faced the sky. Their group stopped just short of passing under it when Archarus turned to them.

'It will be here, at the underbelly of the tower.'

Pelstow scoffed. 'I thought as much. You know this place, don't you?'

'There was a previous expedition.'

'How far did you make it?' Hanwark asked. 'What happened to them?'

'And why didn't it happen to you?' Anora added.

Archarus refused to meet their eyes as he held his silence.

'You need to tell us these things, we need to know it's safe,' Hanwark pressed. 'I won't sanction us going down there if you don't.'

'I can't tell you,' Archarus said through gritted teeth. 'You can't know.'

'Is there a reason why?' Rettic brought himself to ask.

But it wasn't Archarus who answered. He heard a soft gasp at his shoulder and he looked to Anora, a dumbstruck expression on her face.

'I know,' she said. 'That's why I can't go, isn't it?'

'Why can't—?'

Rettic only got two words out before a bark from Archarus cut him off.

'Don't tell him! No one tell him!'

Hanwark seemed to have cottoned on too. 'Oh for the— This is truly sick, Archarus!'

Rettic sensed panic rising in his chest, spurred on by what he'd already felt so far below. 'What, what is it!?' Rettic turned to Pelstow, looking for answers as a dawning horror grew on the Reythurist's face.

'It's a suicide mission, it's pu—'

But before he could get the word out Archarus had closed the distance and thrown a wild punch, hitting him square in the side of the head and sending him into a sprawling heap on the ground. A cry of shock came from Anora. A dagger flashed from Hanwark's holster but Archarus had already danced out of range.

'Do you trust me!?' Archarus barked at Rettic.

'Wh—what?'

Anora was already at Pelstow's side and tending to the sprouting wound at his temple. 'Archarus you can't—'

'Do you trust me, Rettic!?'

'No!' Rettic shouted back. 'And I think you know why!'

Archarus shook his head quickly, a manic grin on his face as he continued to circle away from Hanwark's approach. 'I don't, and that's the only reason this will work. It will be the discovery of a lifetime if it does.' He turned back to Hanwark. 'Let the boy make his choice, I know you've already made yours.'

Hanwark nodded darkly. 'I have. I'm ending this.'

He lunged with the dagger but Archarus was ready for it, dodging left and burning a single green rune in his palm. A surge of magnetism pulsed outwards and the knife was flung form Hanwark's grip. Archarus darted for it, snatching it from the air and holding it to Hanwark's neck before the larger man could react.

'Don't kill him!' Rettic cried out. 'I won't come with you if you kill him!'

'So you will?'

'Only if you tell me what's—'

'You didn't need to be told the purpose of this expedition for you to accept the opportunity so keenly,' Archarus said. 'You knew you were signing up for danger and now is no different.'

'Remember what I told you, boy!' Hanwark hissed. 'You know what this—'

'I know more than you think!'

Archarus shoved Hanwark to the sand and hurled the knife into one of the tower's broken windows. It stopped just before it passed through it, hanging limp in the air.

'Good,' Archarus said breathlessly. 'Come on then. The rest

of you, wait at the camp.'

'I don't think we'll be waiting,' Anora said slowly.

Pelstow groaned —either in agreement or pain— and Rettic couldn't help giving a worried look to Archarus.

'It'll be fine,' he assured him. 'I'll make sure you come out of this alive.'

Silently, Hanwark scooped up Pelstow's limp form and hefted him over his shoulder, regarding Archarus with one last glare before setting off with Anora. Rettic's mind was screaming to go with them, to abandon this madman to his fate. But there was something down there. A machine that should not be controlled. If this was the discovery Archarus was looking for, Rettic needed to stop him.

The underbelly of the tower threw a shade as dark as night with a chill to match. Rettic had to pull his cloak tighter as he followed from a distance of ten paces. Archarus was no longer testing the glass panes like he had that morning. His path was definite, as if he were retracing his steps. Halfway under the tower he crouched low, drawing up to where glass met sand as he beckoned Rettic closer.

He reluctantly obliged, practically having to crawl to avoid his head touching the overhanging glass. Racks of fine machines were arranged in rows inside, either bolted to the floor or completely uninfluenced by the tower's slant. With his imagination running wilder by the second, Rettic thought either were likely.

'Is that what happened with the last expedition?' Rettic asked quietly. 'They knew something Pelstow, Hanwark and Anora knew?'

'Exactly,' Archarus said. 'Something you don't.'

'But why can't I know? What if I already do?' Rettic asked, resisting the urge to tell Archarus what he'd felt last night.

Archarus fixed him with a grimace. 'You wouldn't, you're too young, too bright-eyed. It's something the Academy stopped talking about years ago.'

'Before they got desperate?'

It was a jab adapted from Hanwark, but it only elicited a chuckle from Archarus.

'The Academy of Breggesa isn't desperate. They're full of closed minds that are far too preoccupied with passing that on to the next generation rather than letting someone else make a discovery that would overshadow theirs.'

'And you're not one of these closed minds?'

Archarus shrugged. 'I might be. A man alone cannot tell the colour of their eyes save for a mirror.' He looked to the pane of glass next to them, the reflection making his dull green eyes seem black for a moment. 'Something important to us, isn't it? Without it we wouldn't know what inks and magic we're meant to use.'

'So am I to be your mirror?' Rettic asked.

'No,' he replied. 'I think I am to be yours.'

With an un-gloved hand Archarus pressed slowly against

the glass, his palm passing straight through. He flashed Rettic another mad grin and stood up, disappearing into it with a single step, leaving him alone. Another chance to turn back. But when Rettic glanced up at the glass, there was no sign of Archarus on the other side. He cursed softly under his breath. Maybe he had to trust him.

Rettic copied his actions as precisely as he could, starting with his palm on the cool glass. It felt like pressing into paper and with the lightest pressure he tore through. A cool tingling danced at the skin on his wrist, growing in intensity for a few seconds before something on the other side grasped his hand and wrenched his body through.

There was a thump and a yelp that Rettic could only hope hadn't come from him as he hit the ground in a heap. Carpet prickled against his face like lavishly treated animal furs. It was a dark blue, cool like the rest of the room and somehow free of the dust Rettic had got so used to being coated in.

Archarus pulled him to his feet with ease, brushing down Rettic's cloak as he scanned the room. It took up the entire level of the tower, segmented into sections by more rows of metal shelves that were festooned with some kind of intricate machinery. Rettic could smell all sorts of precious metals hidden away in them, but he was not here to scavenge.

He turned to the glass he'd come through, his stomach jolting from the view. Nothing had really changed. The sand was still where he left it. But it was only now he realised it was him who was standing perfectly upright, a harsh contrast to the crooked horizon outside.

'This is… that isn't—'

'Normal?' Archarus said. 'Try not to think about it.'

CHAPTER FIVE

STAIRS

H E STILL COULDN'T ASSIGN meaning to the endless
aisles of shelves as he and Archarus moved carefully
past their mouths. Each row looked to stretch for a hundred
metres, dark at their middle before being lit in golden light
by the windows at their end. The slanted horizon lay beyond,
seemingly at a different angle every time Rettic observed it.

No inch of space had been left empty on the shelves, a façade
of glass and hyper-machined metal that had been moulded into

the exact same pattern as its neighbours. Why need so many of the same machine?

Rettic made a note of the question to bring it back to the Academy, for duplication was not the general practice of Kretatics when it came to their arcanites. Each one was usually intended to carry out a single, definitive purpose. If that purpose grew, so did the size of the contraption, along with the burden that controlling it would weigh on the creator's mind. Multiple arcanites meant multiple creators, something that was rarely harmonious.

'There's no rust here,' Rettic eventually whispered.

'Why do you think that might be?' Archarus responded.

Rettic hesitated for a moment before risking a few steps down one of the rows. Archarus had asked the question as if it were a test. With what seemed to be at stake, Rettic did not want to fail.

A cooling breeze emanating from grated vents that dotted the low ceiling over the racks, all of which emitted a low whine that Rettic couldn't quite place the source of. The faces of the machines bore strange lenses, minute panels of glass and arrays of tiny mouths with copper teeth that were frozen open in eternal screams. Rettic leaned in, a distinct smell like friction-burnt iron reaching his nose.

'Everything should rust,' Rettic said under his breath. 'It's a fact of life.'

'Why?'

'The water sealed in the air by the extinct Hytharo.'

'These places existed long before that.'

'Maybe these are of metal not of this earth.'

'But they're here,' Archarus said. 'Are they not bound by the laws of this earth?'

Rettic glanced at him, wary of the imperious grin spreading on Archarus' face. 'But what if they're not?'

'Exactly.'

Archarus turned and continued, waving for Rettic to follow. He did so, this time a few more steps behind. Had he answered correctly? Even if he had, it still sprouted more questions. Were these the same machines the otherworldly voice had warned him about? Did Archarus already know about them?

Rettic brushed them from his mind.

He couldn't voice them yet.

An abyss resided at the centre of the floor's interior, ringed on either side by wide stair sets with ornate, almost gaudy white bannisters. These too were carpeted, yet there was no wear at their edges. Rettic glanced up and down the void, finding only endless darkness. What little he could see of the nearest levels showed them identical to this one, another layer of machine replication to puzzle over.

'We haven't time to gawk, Rettic.' Archarus was standing at the foot of the flight of stairs that lead up, his expression patient despite his tone.

'Why are we going up?'

Archarus' grin flashed again. 'You think what we seek lies below?'

Rettic almost swore under his breath for giving his naivety away. 'Common knowledge... well, *folklore* tells that below is...'

'That is where we are going.'

'Going up to go down?' Rettic puzzled.

'Try not to think about it.'

Archarus proceeded up the stairs, his footsteps muffled by the carpet as Rettic hastened to follow. The man's increasingly sinister company was better than no company at all. He paused at each landing for as long as he dared, peering out to the far-off windows as the horizon outside rose closer and closer until the view was engulfed by sand. From there on, the only light came from a dim glow below each step's edge and the occasional distant flash that emanated from deep in the machine racks.

'This place really is quite the wonder,' Rettic said as they climbed, doing his best to keep his voice innocent. 'How did you know this would lead us below the sands?'

'It's a good question,' Archarus replied.

Rettic held his tongue for a few heartbeats before throwing caution to the wind. Did he know? Maybe it was time to throw caution to the wind.

'Is it because you made it this far on your last expedition?'

'We made it further.'

'But there were no reports in the Academy of Breggesa's archives,' Rettic replied. 'No records, nothing.'

Archarus scoffed. 'The archives only contain certainties, Rettic. Facts that scholars are foolish or gullible enough to commit to paper.'

'As if they were closed minds?'

'Indeed,' he continued. 'A great deal of study requires uncertainty. It requires wonder, questioning and variation. It's very difficult to argue with what is carved in stone, yet from a fresh set of eyes a new idea can be created.'

'But what new ideas are there to be had?'

'How am I to know?' Archarus stopped at the next landing, breathing heavily from the climb and beckoning Rettic to his side. 'If you peer down from where we came, what do you see?'

'Nothing, it's too dark.'

'So how could you know what's down there without seeing it? Know that there's anything down there at all?'

Rettic hesitated. It seemed like a trick question. 'I'd have to create light somehow, like a torch I could throw.'

'But if I told you what lay below and you trusted that answer completely, would you be likely to go confirm it?'

'If I trusted you... I mean your answer... No, I wouldn't,' Rettic said.

'And if you'd seen it, recalled it perfectly and written it down, would you ever have reason to reconsider it?'

'I wouldn't,' Rettic repeated. He paused, looking back down into the void again. 'That's why you can't tell me what happened, isn't it? Or what we're looking for? Because you've seen it and you cannot change what you've seen. Is that the kind of magic we're dealing with?'

His breath finally caught, Archarus nodded and continued up the stairs. 'When I was your age the Academy of Breggesa was just as young. They thought this way. Anything studying was worth studying again by a fresh mind that could prescribe another meaning to it. It was a time before the archives when knowledge could be fluid. It was the way study was carried out on the runes that make up our axioms. Yet there came a day when our leaders viewed it as wasteful. Dangerous, perhaps.'

'Is what you want me to see dangerous?' Rettic asked carefully.

'Of course it is,' Archarus replied. 'A new idea is the most dangerous thing of all.'

Rettic's mind chewed on the concept like a fatty piece of meat as they continued up the stairs. He'd always trusted the archives as complete. A true record of every study the Academy had undertaken, curated so those beyond them could build further.

But if what Archarus said was true, how much was missing? Was what Rettic learnt so far been an erroneous product of conclusions made by half-erased histories? And just how much knowledge was hidden in the minds of those who'd studied before him?

Perhaps Archarus was right in thinking a fresh mind more valuable than a full one. The others of the expedition had been afraid, repelled by something they'd learnt long ago, something they trusted only because they'd been told to trust it. But they hadn't heard the voice from deep below.

The thought of it made Rettic miss a step. What if the unintentional act of hearing it had closed his mind? It was similar to what Archarus had mentioned about the first studies of runes and axioms. Each rune that made up an axiom could mean a number of different words, making different statements depending on the intention of those who called them into action, yet many learned of each one only by their singular effect for which it was practical in their lives. Any different or new meanings were all but locked off to them until they could see it demonstrated in practice.

Rettic knew he controlled machines. He knew that there was a machine down here that could control him. He knew that he must not control it. But would that be enough to seal his fate?

His mind buzzed louder and louder with the concept until the stairs finally ran out. The metal racks were absent, the carpeted floor replaced by a single slab of perfectly polished granite. The ceiling was higher, festooned with strange, blackened thorns that lanced down at terrifying angles.

Elaborate sculptures hung from invisible wires, human-like forms that were frozen in motion. They dived and weaved in a wild scramble to get away from the structure's yawning façade of shattered glass. More structures lay beyond it, just as decayed and illuminated by the orange glow of light that trickled in from afar.

The glass lay coated across every flat surface within sight. Rettic crouched down as he examined it. Each shard was no larger than his thumbnail, most practically sand at this point. It made the orange light glitter across what it struck, giving the impression that everything was layered with hot coals. Despite the perceived heat, the air was cooler than before.

A mess of footprints lay before them. Rows of waist-height marble slabs that formed an aisle-like path through the atrium. Five sets forward, one set back. Rettic glanced to Archarus.

'You made it further. With the last expedition, I mean.'

'What if I told you I didn't?'

Rettic cleared his throat to stop himself from scoffing. 'Let's not delude ourselves of these footprints, they clearly—'

'But what if they weren't mine?' Archarus said. 'What if they were another's?'

'Then I would worry for a group who came in with five and left only with one,' Rettic said coldly. 'Did you leave them down here to die?'

'It's much more complicated than that.'

'I need to know the truth,' he spat back.

'The truth is a dangerous thing, Rettic.'

'More dangerous than the idea that led to it?'

After a moment Archarus chuckled. 'Beaten at my own game. You'll have your truth, but it's something you'll need to see for yourself.'

He started toward the atrium's exit, stopping after a few steps when he realised Rettic was still bolted in place.

'I think I know what you are,' Rettic said. 'What you're trying to become.'

Archarus raised an eyebrow, infuriatingly calm.

'A shadow dancer.'

'Not quite,' Archarus said. 'Not yet. There's so much more you don't know. Things that would stop me from becoming that.'

Archarus turned and began walking, expecting Rettic to follow, but he still remained.

'A machine that controls life,' Rettic called after him. 'A machine we must not control!'

He halted again and Rettic stormed to his side, grabbing his shoulder and turning him briskly to see the shame and defeat in his eyes.

'So you know...'

Rettic nodded. 'There was a voice down there. I lied when I said I couldn't repair the Gyurian Axle. I managed it. I found a resonance and it spoke to me, but there was so much more. Thousands that were identical and almost... almost mindless.'

'I've... I've never heard a voice.'

Rettic's eyes shot wide. How did he know more than Archarus?

'Your help isn't for me,' he continued. 'Whatever burden I carry, whatever the Axle sensed... It's my fate alone. I didn't lie to you in suggesting my last expedition didn't die. But what they've become...'

'It's why you need my help,' Rettic said slowly. 'Because you couldn't save them, you didn't know how because you'd exhausted every option!'

Archarus nodded as a tear blossomed at the corner of his eye. But instead of fading in the tiny puff of steam it should have, it rolled down his cheek, the first drop of water Rettic had ever witnessed outside an extraction pump or a well-sealed vial. Rettic reached out to his cheek to wipe it away out of an almost ancient instinct, the wetness feeling impossible on his fingertip.

'You don't have to help me,' Archarus said. 'I wouldn't trust myself to. But can you help them?'

'I don't think I could live with the choice if I were to make it.'

CHAPTER SIX

BUNKER

KEEPING HIS DISTANCE, RETTIC followed Archarus beyond the tower's shattered walls and into the cavern. More towers stretched to a high ceiling of smooth and dark rock, piercing it like spears before undoubtedly breaching the sands above. They were so densely packed that they obscured the source of the strange orange glow, despite not a single one still possessing a wall or window unharmed by decay or destruction.

The untouched and ancient debris now littered the network of black stone pathways. It ranged from a fine powder of crystalline glass masquerading as the remains of a sandstorm to piles of jagged concrete and un-rusted metal that turned their path into a murky trench. Rettic had long dismissed all advice of avoiding the shadows. The prickling warmth of the orange light seemed far more dangerous.

Rettic suppressed a shiver as they passed a narrow alley formed between two towers, the originator of the orange glow coming into sight. It was a miniature sun, a thousand times dimmer, colder and closer, yet still suspended in the air at the centre of the cavern, its solid surface the only work of glass that had survived whatever cataclysm had wracked this place.

Archarus' path suddenly took a detour and Rettic struggled to suppress his suspicion that he was being led into a trap before they stopped at a crumbling lookout. It was at the heart of a long-collapsed tower and represented the first chance Rettic had at taking in the scene from on high.

He'd wondered why the ruins exposed above stood as circles, vacant in the middle, but now he could see it was because its roots were just the same. Tiers of the city descended towards the very centre where the imitation sun hovered, the higher ground held back by cliff-like walls of banded metal and stone. While Rettic's first sights of the place had been of destruction, they'd been pristine compared to the two inner-most tiers.

Rubble and scrap flowed like dunes, clearing only as they

encroached on the stout grey bunker which the sun was positioned over. It had no windows, barely any corners and no sign of the rash of parasitic-looking metal instruments that infected the surrounding towers.

'That's the place,' Archarus said quietly from his side.

'But... but there's no door.'

Archarus didn't answer, instead setting off down the path of rubble. Rettic tailed him, having to carefully negotiate his way through to avoid impaling himself on jagged rebar. Stopping at the tier before the bottom, Rettic called his guide to a halt. The wreck of a machine —almost an arcanite in its form— lay nearby.

'What is that thing?'

'Dead.'

Rettic moved cautiously to inspect one in case this was another lie. It was twenty metres long, larger than any arcanite he'd seen —spare for the fortress of Revance— and so much more complex. Its form mimicked that of a snake, with a hide of interlocking scales that were burnt and pockmarked from battle. As he proceeded along its length, he passed rending wounds that'd been inflicted on its underside. Guts of wires, flexible piping and oozing silver liquid spilled out, the liquid itself trembling with each of Rettic's footsteps.

'Don't touch the flux!' Archarus said quickly. 'The... the silver fluid, I—'

'It has a name?' Rettic snapped back. 'How do you know it

has a name?'

He didn't get an answer and moved further along the beast's body, heeding Archarus' warning despite his curiosity. The machine's fearsome face bore complex arrays of glass for eyes and what looked like gun barrels for teeth, though Rettic had never seen something so refined before.

The few man portable hand cannons he'd had the misfortune to be in earshot of when they were fired had been unwieldy creations, as long as a man was tall and just as heavy. But this creature's weapons ran only a few inches from its mouth, the loading mechanism seemingly hidden beyond its jaw. Rettic glanced back to the silver ooze. Maybe these weren't weapons for solid slugs at all.

'Is this what killed them? Your last expedition crew?'

He nodded.

'Then why did you tell me they aren't dead?'

'Use an axiom,' he said calmly. 'Send out a sweep. Find them. Feel them.'

Archarus held up his palm, revealing a single green rune as it burned white hot, then he simply vanished. A wave of invisible energy tremored through Rettic's bones, the kind he'd been expecting from a Kretatic's scan of their surroundings, but this time it shook him to the core. Was this some kind of trick like he'd played on the others?

A dull crunch of crushing glass echoed through the undercity, then another, just like footsteps. Rettic crept closer to where Archarus had been, the ground that'd been at his feet now free of glass, and each tinkling of the fragments accompanied by what looked like a boot-print's impression that formed a trail towards the bunker.

Rettic withdrew his ink and a brush from his pouch, daubing runes of his own onto his wrist. It was reckless, but now there was no time for caution. Anything to save him from another second of being alone in the undercity. The runes seared in his palm and a second later every inch of his skin was doing the same, pulling and stretching until his bones felt like they were about to burst out through his flesh.

Suddenly he was on the ground, gasping for air and scrambling across glass as his sight came back to him in pinpricks of light. A set of hands grabbed him, hauling him to his feet despite his thrashing attempts at fighting them off before he realised it was Archarus. Rettic broke free of his grip, staggering a few paces before he could catch himself.

'Why didn't you—'

'Tell you?' Archarus interrupted. 'I needed you to find out the same way I did. The same way I lost sight of my expedition when that war machine attacked them.'

'So then where are...'

Rettic's words trailed off as he turned away from Archarus. They were still in the undercity, but it was different. Newer. Intact. The orange light had turned blue, the crumbled tiers around them restored along with the constructs which had stood upon them. Shallow trenches ran between them, likely once filled with that mythical water people were sometimes lucky to find in places like these.

The only flecks of glass left on the ground were the ones which had lain at his and Archarus' feet when they'd used their axioms. All else was now back upon the pristine walls of the towers where they belonged. Even the mechanical beasts were absent.

'Are we in the same place?'

'I've long wondered,' Archarus said. 'I believed this bunker would hold the answer, but instead it held something else.'

'But it's...'

The bunker was different. Shinier, more angled, even bearing a door which Archarus now stood next to. This was the only place where signs of battle damage lingered. A thousand pockmarks speckled their surroundings, the remnants of a bloodbath which the defenders had long succumbed to. Rettic glanced around again. Why had the fight been here?

The war machines, the devastation, it had all remained in the version of the city they'd walked into, yet these ancient attackers had learnt of the way into this one. Or had there been two battles happening at once? And what of the lands above, would Rettic even be in the same realm he'd descended from if he were to leave now? The questions made his head swirl as he turned and turned again to make sense of it.

'Try not to think about it,' Archarus said. 'One city was

saved, one was not. The magic of those-of-glass could have split the two in their own defence, but the tale of how or why they did this is not the one we were searching for.'

'Then what were you looking for?'

'What they were hiding.'

Archarus entered the bunker and in spite of himself, Rettic followed. The blue light dared to only stray in for a few steps, soon replaced by the green glow of Archarus' torch. The concrete walls were narrow, only marked with shallow alcoves that were also scarred from battle. A dead end of steel was up ahead, but Archarus had already found a mechanism to split an entrance through it by the time Rettic had caught up.

Another alcove appeared beyond, bathing them with yellow light as Archarus beckoned him in. There was barely room for the two to stand, but before Rettic could have any second thoughts the steel walls slid shut, sealing them in with a pneumatic hiss. Archarus was already fiddling with another control pad, a grid of white buttons that flashed green as he pressed each one. Once all were pressed, they simultaneously blinked again.

The ground lurched and suddenly they were descending, yet the means which carried them were unseen and unheard. Rettic had to brace himself against a corner, but Archarus seemed unbothered by it. Maybe even familiar.

'This isn't magic, is it?' Rettic said. 'This is technology, built by those-of-glass. How could you know of its workings?'

Archarus didn't meet his eye, still facing the steel walls as the chamber rattled around them. 'Something else I've long wondered. An instinct, a vision, perhaps even an unseen message that those-of-glass could drop into one's mind like an infectious thought if they wished. But I remember after I'd fought the beast I was drawn here.'

'How did you best it?'

Archarus looked at him, struggling to hide a smirk. 'Come now, Rettic. We are both kin of the Kretatic. It was made of metal. Our domain.'

'You controlled it,' Rettic said breathlessly. 'And the liquid inside, the one which you said not to touch—'

'Molten flux. Liquid metal.' Archarus took a deep and shuddering breath. 'It wasn't what we'd been searching for. But I think it's what we were meant to find.'

The motion of the chamber slowed and Rettic felt like his bones were too big again. Another hiss and the doors slid open, another darkened corridor stretching before them as stale and putrid air invaded his lungs. Doors lined it where the alcoves were, all flung open, yet only one at the far end of the corridor spilled light.

CHAPTER SEVEN

CONTROL

RETTIC STEPPED OUT INTO the corridor first, shooting a warning glare back at Archarus and snatching the green torch from his limp hand. If he were to save the lost expedition, then it could not be by the lead of the man who caused this untold harm in the first place. His boots did not echo as they clacked off the stone floor, yet Archarus' following footsteps created the impression well enough.

The middling light the torch provided was no match for the

darkness of each room he attempted to shine it into. Only a few feet of tightly arranged hexagonal tiles the width of his foot would be illuminated. Fear of the unknown that lay beyond withered his temptation to stray from the corridor. Before stepping into the path of the yellow light at the end of the corridor, he stashed the torch and turned back to Archarus.

'Is this where you brought them?'

'After we encountered the beast? Yes.'

'And?'

'I had to leave them there.'

Rettic had to suppress a moan of frustration. 'I need the truth, Archarus. Everything. What happened to them, *in detail*.'

'Molten flux. That's what happened to them.'

'What did it do?'

A grimace crossed Archarus' expression as he reached for his collar, pulling it back to reveal his pallid chest. While his face and hands had been tanned, rugged and worn, here the skin was thin and pale. It was translucent to the point it exposed the veins running beneath it, along with the silver that tinted them.

'I was lucky,' Archarus muttered as he righted his tunic. 'It's why I told you not to touch it. Because it's not just a metal.'

'A machine that controls life,' Rettic breathed. 'That's what the voice said. The voice you said you didn't hear!'

'I was telling you the truth for that,' Archarus replied. 'I wish I'd heard it.'

'But would you have heeded the warning?'

'Have you?'

Rettic barely realised his fists were clenched at his side. Even as he relaxed his straining knuckles, his hands still shook. Something in the air was infecting his throat, forming as a lump far heavier than panic alone could create. He'd been a fool, the exact same fool as Archarus, one he was so damn sure he was avoiding becoming.

But now it was too late.

He was in too deep.

Rettic stepped into the light and through the doorway it emanated from. The chamber was massive, circular and tiled floor-to-ceiling in the same hexagonal tiles as the other rooms. Their dull white sheen was spattered with long-dried blood.

Countless cots were arrayed in a perfect grid through the room with little more than a foot in between, all engulfed by a forest of metal stands and other instruments. Wires reached like vines for the ceiling, coiling tightly into the labyrinth of twisting pipes that ran overhead. The only time the network to tubes split was to allow for a hanging glow bulb of yellow light, each one hovering perfectly over a cot.

Rettic suddenly registered what lay on the cots. A small gasp escaped him. He couldn't help it. At first glance he'd thought of them as corpses, the remains of those-of-glass, but if that were the case they'd be nothing but bone powder after the eons said to have passed.

He risked a few more steps to the nearest, his eyes wide with horror at the sight of full, tanned skin, the breath that ever so gently moved their chest hidden under the clean white gown, and their open, staring eyes that were fixed on the ceiling. Silver swirled in the whites with no sign of the iris and everything else that should have gone with it. It was a rough count, but there could be hundreds of bodies like this one here, thousands if the other rooms contained the same.

'They're alive,' Rettic breathed. 'They're all alive, aren't they? Controlled but alive. I heard them. Thousands of resonances, all the same... It was all these people.'

'A Kretatic without their own resonance is a Kretatic without their own mind. The same looks to be true for others.'

'A machine that controls life,' Rettic repeated under his breath. He kept saying it as he walked among the cots, living burials for a people long past their time. 'But why? Why does it need control!?'

'Because to control life is to create it,' Archarus replied.

Rettic looked back to him, meeting his dark gaze as he realised Archarus was still stood in the doorway. A silence held them both in place until Rettic broke it.

'Don't.'

'You can save them,' Archarus said as he stepped back through the door. 'You just *need* to.'

Rettic kicked into a sprint, only making it two steps before a pair of metal barriers slammed shut in front of his former mentor. He kicked and screamed at the door, pounding at it for what good it would do, but each time his open palm bounced off it, there was no doubting the resonance now held in the metal.

Tiring quickly, Rettic descended into a slump against the wall, cursing himself for having ever trusted the bastard. Hopefully Anora and Hanwark had managed to nurse Pelstow back to health and set off. If he were to die alone down here, Archarus deserved the exact same fate.

Where the bastard got the idea that the best way to help his former expedition was to trap him down here was beyond Rettic. What'd he even meant by *needing* to save them?

Another wave of panic forced Rettic to his feet as he scanned the room. What if they were hidden among the cots, just one of the many he'd have to search through? How would he even understand what needed to be done, let alone carry it out?

He began making his way among them, scanning their lifeless faces, their clothes, anything for a hint of the world he'd come from that would differentiate them from the world of those-of-glass. But he hadn't needed to look at the cots at all. Rettic stopped in the centre of the room, spotting a huddle of four figures standing at the far side.

Standing.

Dread rooted him to the spot, begging him to run, to cry out to see if they'd save him or even to hear they'd met the same fate. Yet if they'd been able to answer, would they not have asked the same of him? Rettic approached slowly, but they didn't react to his presence. The four faced the wall and each other, standing so close their shoulders touched through their torn and scorched cloaks. Their skin was like Archarus', pallid and silvered, the veins almost throbbing as the molten flux pumped through.

'Four,' Rettic muttered to himself. 'An expedition of five. One survived...'

One had a satchel at their back and Rettic reached for it like a pickpocket would, gingerly slipping the flap open and withdrawing what felt like a glass vial. He'd been expecting it to be full of runic ink, but only a single silver drop sat in it. Rettic twisted the vial to read the scrawled label.

Machine. Inert until shook.

Rettic turned the vial again, just in time to see the drop expand to fill the entire container. There must have been ten times as much of it now. But how had they known to call it "machine?" Hanwark said that expeditions generally only took one Kretatic, which meant none of these four could be...

'You lying fucker!' Rettic hissed through his teeth.

Archarus *had* heard the voice! Warning and all, and he'd still come down here! Then seen fit to try again, using him as a fresh mind because of nothing more than his insane philosophy of learning through sheer ignorance! But now Rettic had cottoned onto what he'd been scheming. Now he could get one step ahead!

If only he could work out how.

It took some debating, but he eventually placed his hand gently on the nearest figure's shoulder. They turned automatically at his touch, the man's mindless stare now stretching out across the cots.

Automind.

A sick giggle rose up in Rettic's chest at the word. It was so dehumanising, so... so objectifying for what had once been an entire person, a life.

Now they were nothing. Another vessel for the mysterious liquid machine that filled their veins. Giving a name to what they now were was the least he could do.

The other autominds turned just as easily, revealing the savage wounds that tattered their fronts. Molten flux oozed slowly instead of blood, barely congealing to fill the torn skin and the slightest jostle would make the silvery liquid spill across the floor. Rettic leapt back the first time it happened, watching in a sickening awe as the metal cauterised in the wound. At his feet, the puddle spread until the thin guttering between each hexagonal tile stopped it.

The temptation to poke it was immense, but finding the same fate as all the others here held Rettic back. If the molten flux kept spreading like that, it wouldn't be long until this whole room was brimming with it.

He crossed back to the other side of the room, running his hands along the door and the walls around it. Archarus' resonance still resided in the former, but the walls were nothing but concrete, or stone, or whatever those-of-glass had made this place from. Lattices of iron reinforced it, buried deep but still close enough that Rettic could feel it. Maybe even control it.

The feverish madness of the idea took hold as Rettic found his ink and a brush, etching out the runes in record time before any semblance of caution could stop him. Once they'd burned in his hand he slammed his palm to the wall, willing his resonance through stone until he could feel the metal within. He clamped onto it, following each intersecting piece of the lattice in five different directions to find more and more until it felt like he'd engulfed the entire chamber.

They were now his bones, the inner walls his skin, and he squeezed at them, something distant in his ears roaring in pain before it faded, yet the stone refused to yield. He pushed again, another scream lancing out, but this time he realised it was his own! Agony suddenly wracked his body, all sense of control lost as he trembled into a pathetic ball on the ground. It was too much to control, Rettic thought as his vision began to fade, too much for his tiny mind alone.

But what if it didn't have to be his mind?

He awoke with an incoherent shout sometime later. He didn't know how long exactly, but judging by the tender bruise he could feel on his cheek, it had been enough time for the impact of his fall to blossom into something nasty under his skin. A pang of hunger growled in his belly and he doubted anything down here would be edible.

Rettic found his feet in a daze, his vision swirling as he looked around the room. As far as he could see, nothing had yet changed, but he still didn't want to wait around to see it happen. Not that he currently had much of a choice.

His last thought before he'd fallen reappeared in his mind. He glanced to the nearest cot and the automind still lying on it. Perhaps their mind could aid his? The bed was on wheels and Rettic dragged it over to the door as another internal conflict raged within.

You control machines.

This machine will control life.

Do not control it.

He paused, his ink-loaded brush hovering above his wrist. What had the voice meant by "life?" Was it his own? Others? Either way, it was too late to stop it. Archarus was already infected by the molten flux, maybe even maddened by it. Another prong of dread split from Rettic's thoughts. What would Archarus do once he opened the door? Would he fight back? Would he even consider letting Rettic go?

He drew two copies of the same axiom onto his wrist, four runes in each, designed to overpower a lingering resonance left by another Kretatic upon a piece of metal. It was not something he'd practised often, as invading another's influence over an arcanite was an action bound to start a brawl, yet in the circumstances he'd do anything to give Archarus a solid punch in the jaw.

The first axiom readied itself in his palm as he held it over the automind, his hand only an inch from its forehead. A strange prickling sensation had already taken his hand, perhaps the influence of the molten flux flowing just below their skin. He wasn't used to flesh feeling like that and he prayed he never would be. Rettic clenched his eyes shut as the last rune burned and then the exhilarating rush of control crashed over him like a wave.

The automind's body sprayed out before his senses, their veins a tangled tapestry of roots for to Rettic dart through, every drop of the liquid metal instantly his, along with every inch of skin and pump of blood, a second body suddenly outside his own. He returned his focus to the corpse's mind, finding it as an empty palace that dwarfed his own, unbothered by the trivialities of living and breathing, for the flux itself bore that burden. It was like walking through the undercity again, yet the space was clear of skyscrapers, of anything at all!

Rettic sped the next axiom up his palm, hurling it at the door just as it seared hot. Suddenly the empty space in his twin minds was occupied by Archarus' resonance. It appeared in the distance, taking the form of a dark and featureless silhouette. Rettic watched carefully, its movement in his mind quivering and halting as it neared.

But before it could touch him, he felt his own blazing resonance burst forth as a dazzling light from his chest and the figure was vanquished. The door became his, the sound of it crashing open impossibly distant. It still rang in his ears as he withdrew from the empty city and back into his body.

Archarus was before him, pain and shock frozen on his face as he reeled from the defeat, falling to the floor as Rettic reluctantly relinquished his influence on the door, but still keeping the automind under his control.

'Did you, was it—?'

'No,' Rettic said. 'I don't know. I don't want to know. But I didn't save them. I can't.'

'Then how did you take the door?' Archarus stammered. 'I... I felt you... It was like being crushed by the world itself. No Kretatic's resonance is so... so...'

Rettic shook his head. 'It wasn't just mine.' He turned to his automind. It didn't even take a conscious thought for it to sit up and climb out of the cot. 'It was theirs.'

A sick horror embraced him as he looked out over the rest of the autominds, the hundreds of empty vessels just waiting to be controlled. Tools, weapons, whatever they were, there would be no limit to the power one could have. They'd be able to create an arcanite the size of the walking fortress of Revance, maybe something larger!

They could control all life.

A soft groan escaped his lips as another wave of realisation hit him. That was what the voice meant. The molten flux itself wasn't the danger. He was. Archarus, hell, any other Kretatic who found their way down here wouldn't be able to resist the lure of this much power. And the only way to get more of it was with corpses. Thousands upon thousands of corpses until every speck of metal and life was under one's control.

Rettic looked back to him as he got to his feet, the same dawning horror on Archarus' face as his halting walk took him deeper into the chamber. Rettic stepped back into the corridor, withdrawing his brush and ink one last time.

'How did you do it?' Archarus babbled, standing at the centre of the chamber. 'How!?'

Rettic looked up from the freshly painted axiom on his wrist. His arm was just out of sight through the doorframe and Archarus hadn't noticed. 'I can't tell you.'

'But you must! I'll die if you don't!'

'We'll all die if I do.'

The axiom burned in Rettic's palm and he touched it to the doorframe, only catching a fraction of Archarus' desperate scream before it slammed shut. Rettic closed his eyes, counting under his breath.

A bash of energy clanged against the door as Rettic's resonance was attacked. Archarus' dark form reappeared in the strange, empty city the automind had created for him, but it felt like little more than the thrashing of a child's tantrum. Nothing but wild, flailing swings that they both knew were futile.

As he held it back, Rettic assigned control of the battle to the automind, bit by bit until it was barely a memory in his own head.

Maybe he should have tried to finish Archarus, just to be sure, but as Rettic walked back down the corridor, he told himself he didn't have to. Even if Archarus escaped, his own curiosity would be an impregnable prison.

CHAPTER EIGHT

RISING

STANDING BEFORE THE CLAUSTROPHOBIC chamber that had brought him so deep, Rettic could already feel Archarus' attacks at his resonance waning in both strength and resolve. Perhaps he'd given up. Maybe he'd accepted his fate as inevitable. Just another closed mind like those he'd railed against.

He stepped into the chamber, his finger shaking as it hovered over the button-strew panel that Archarus had been all too familiar with. Before he resolved to press one, the doors slid shut and the floor lurched, descending once more.

By now Rettic was far too weary to panic. When doors slid open after only a few seconds, another dim corridor stretched before him. This one was shorter, a lonely door ajar at the end. A white glow emanated from it, calling Rettic in and he obeyed.

It swung open before he could touch it and he stepped into the room beyond. Almost all the space was filled by an enormous bed pressed against the back wall. The skeleton of a man three times the size of him lay there. Their bones were held in place not by pulsing lengths of molten flux that spanned the gaps like a thick ichor. Coloured wires were threaded throughout as a replacement for long decayed veins, splitting out of the body to snake into the dormant machines on either side of the bed.

Rettic couldn't believe his eyes. What Kretatics saw in resonances was usually the stuff of metaphor, a mind's way of conceptualising a feeling into a clear thought.

But the bones were real.

And if they'd spoken to him...

With a trembling hand Rettic moved closer, laying it on the leg of the giant. A resonance flowed through him, a surge of fatigue that eclipsed his own. One that could only come from the living.

It was old.

Old and tired.

'I didn't listen to you,' Rettic whispered.

And yet, you heard me.

'But is that enough?'

That is for you to decide.

'And Archarus?'

He did not listen.

'And he'll likely die for it,' Rettic said.

He removed his hand, looking to the giant's skull only to see a pair of silver orbs staring back. Nothing but molten flux. Perhaps this being was the first, the origin, even, of molten flux. Rettic shook the thought from his head. He knew too much already and finding out more would only lead him to Archarus' fate.

Rettic castigated himself for it as he turned and walked back down the corridor. This entity could have been from those-of-glass, a miraculously living link to the past that could reveal the answers to so much which the Academy of Breggesa pondered. But could they be trusted with the knowledge?

He allowed himself one last glimpse of the colossal skeleton before the doors of the elevating chamber slid shut. The room began to rise. Rettic chewed his lip as he looked at the mechanism panel in front of him, not a single light showing on it. What if he or even Archarus had never even controlled it? Was it the flux? The skeleton? Even those-of-glass?

When Rettic was finally back on the surface of the undercity, it was on the pristine side. To make his path more familiar, he painted and burnt a single-runed axiom. His bones stretched again, the blue light turned to orange, and he was bizarrely relieved to be surrounded by devastation.

He picked his way through the debris carefully, lingering near the downed war beast before resolving to not pilfer a sample of its workings. What lay down here should be forgotten, he thought to himself as he trekked back down the stairs that took him to the surface. A glowing sunset soon pieced through the glass walls of the tower's innards.

Rettic was too exhausted to celebrate his survival and by the time he'd found the right pane of glass to step through and haplessly fall onto the sand, even the sun had grown impatient of waiting for him to emerge. The only reason he could summon in his mind to return to this accursed tower was if he toted enough explosive crash-powder to level it.

A lone tent remained at the centre of the ruin, without even a mark in the sand to show the rest had ever been there. At least the others had left him something. His and Archarus' packs and a stash of rations lay inside, along with a trio of scrawled notes. Rettic had to squint to read them in the ebbing moonlight.

One was addressed to both himself and Archarus, one to Archarus, and one to him alone. He unfurled the first and recognised Pelstow's hand upon it. As bothersome as the man had been, his talent with a pencil was immaculate. Shame it was wasted as only a comparison to insult Rettic's own scribbled words.

For Rettic and Archarus.

If the both of you have made it back, then know we have left without you. If you have both survived, then know what awaits on return to the Academy will not be congratulatory. What you may have discovered, or failed to do so, is not worth a punch in the face or the meddling with forces long cautioned by anyone with half a mind.

Pelstow.

The next was Hanwark's, a great deal messier and seemingly enraged, judging by the smudging of graphite across it.

I knew this would happen.

What you have done to that poor boy is wrong.

Expect the same if you ever show your face.

Rettic placed it down with a low whistle. Had this message been delivered in person it would've been immediately acted upon. He turned to the third, this time from Anora, likely written for the event that he was forced to come back without Archarus and the desperate circumstances that would have led to it.

RETTIC.

DO NOT SEEK US.

FORGET WHAT YOU SAW.

TAKE NOTHING WITH YOU.

YOUR SURVIVAL IS NOT A MARK OF HONOUR.

ANORA.

Rettic read this message three times over, his throat closing over as his vision blurred the words into shapeless blots. What had he done? What fate had Archarus levelled on him? He rummaged in his satchel, finding the vial of molten flux and holding it to the night sky. The moonlight caught the silver, making it glint ominously as it sloshed.

He couldn't dump it into the sands, it would probably multiply and swallow the world whole. There was no way he could make another trip back to the undercity to bury it, either. Not while there was still a chance of re-encountering Archarus. All he could do was guard it, he resolved, study it and learn how to destroy it.

Even if it took a lifetime.

PRONUNCIATION GUIDE AND GLOSSARY

(If a term or pronunciation is not included here, it has either been omitted to avoid spoilers, is not worth mentioning, or would be pronounced as read. Bolded parts of pronunciations indicate emphasis on that particular syllable.)

Characters:

- Rettic: *Ret-tic*

- Archarus: *Ar-**cha**-rus*

- Hanwark: *Han-wark (the "wark" sounds like "quark")*

- Anora: *A-nor-a*

- Pelstow: *Pel-stow*

Magic:

- Ink:

  - Concocted from impossibly rare liquid water and a number of other ingredients, ink is used to draw runes onto the skin of one who wants to use magic. Each vial is specially brewed depending on which type of magic they were born to use.

- Runes:

  - Each piece of magic, or axiom, is made up of a number of runes. A single rune will mean a word, or a number of words, which are often determined by the intention of who is using it at the time.

- Axioms:

  - An axiom is the resulting magic itself, a statement of words summoned into the world to change it. It can also refer to a sequence of runes that are ready on someone's skin.

- Arcanite: *Arc-an-ite*

  - An arcanite can refer to any piece of magically bound metal created by a Kretatic's axioms. A Kretatic can use these for many purposes, be it as weapons, beasts of burden or other ingenious uses. While under their control, a Kretatic must commit a portion of their mind to the metal to control it. In

    return, they can sense things through the metal as if

    it was their own jesh. The larger and more complex the arcanite is, the greater the stress that is placed on a Kretatic's mind.

- Paralict: *Par-a-lict*

  - A paralict is an unnatural ob-ect often found in the ruins of thosezofzglass. They carry bi2arre and incomprehensible magics with them and are as dangerous and forbidden as they are valuable.

- Fracture:

  - The name given to areas of anomalous phenomena usually contained within the ruins of those-of-glass.

Places:

- The Droughtlands:

  - The never-ending dunes of the Droughtlands are sparsely populated and even less settled. Long drained of any liquid water, its inhabitants live a scavenger's life, hydrated by an ancient act of magic performed by the extinct Hytharo that locked the water into the air.

- Breggesa: *Bre-gges-a*

  - The largest city in the Droughtlands, an enormous trade hub at the crossroads of several regions and home of the Academy of Breggesa.

- Revance: *Re-vance*

  - Revance is the gargantuan walking fortress that wanders across the Droughtlands, both as a cargo hauler and as a mercenary outfit. Despite being one gigantic arcanite, its creator and controller are still unknown.

- The Ruins of those-of-glass:

  - The mysterious towers poking out of the dunes in clusters across the Droughtlands are seen as places of unpredictable danger, yet this doesn't stop brave and foolish souls from venturing into their depths in search of powerful treasures or secret magics.

Peoples:

- Kretatic: **Kre**-*ta-tic*

  - Born with green eyes, these peoples use their magic to magnetically bind scrap metal into arcanites.

- Reythurist: *Rey-thur-**ist***

  - With blue eyes, they have a keen sense of the air around them, their magic giving them the ability to manipulate it in unexpected and often deadly ways.

- Curiktic: *Cu-rik-**tic***

  - Drawing the roots of their magic from the ever-burning sun, yellow-eyed Curiktics can summon blinding light or blazing fire, the latter of which either causing or cauterising wounds.

- Hytharo: ***Hy-thar**-o (The "Hy" sounds like "high", and "thar" almost sounds a bit like "their", but with more of an "a" sound.)*

  - Extinct for eons, the H^yt*haro*—

- The Academy of Breggesa:

  - An organisation headquartered in the city of its namesake dedicated to research into magic, both that which is known and long forgotten. They are as clandestine as they are ruthless.

- Those-of-glass:

  - The name that the people of the Droughtlands to those who built the various forbidden ruins that are scattered across the dunes. Little else is known about them, other than their magic being impossibly different from what is known.

ABOUT THE AUTHOR

Jonathan Weiss is an Australian Fantasy & Science Fiction author of The Flux Catastrophe and The First Hytharo series. Ever since being a small boy he hunted for the best way to tell stories, dabbling in stop motion before eventually finding a passion for writing as a teenager. More than a decade later he'd gathered a bachelor's degree of Journalism and a career in commercial cloud sales, yet they were never as satisfying as writing.

With the support of his artist wife and a trio of pet budgies, he's now dedicated himself to a full-time career as an author. When not writing, Jonathan can be found reading, working through the never-ending queue of un-painted Warhammer 40,000 models and attempting to fit far too much food on his tiny barbeque.

Also By

The Flux Catastrophe

RISING FLUX: The Prequel Novella to Molten Flux (March 2023)

MOLTEN FLUX (June 2023)

BLAZING FLUX (April 2024)

The First Hytharo

THE HYTHARO REDUX (October 2023)

Check out my website: **jonathanweiss.com.au** to find more great books that've since been published!

And don't forget to leave a review online, either on Goodreads or from where you purchased this book, it helps massively in getting this book in front of other readers, meaning you'll have more people to talk to about it!

Looking to see the outcome of Rettic's discovery? Then make sure to pick up MOLTEN FLUX, the first book of The Flux Catastrophe! As a bonus, the first chapter is included on the very next page for your enjoyment.

As the freshest conscript aboard the walking fortress of Revance, Ryza forges a name for himself in battle. The enemy are the smelters, bandits that trade in reanimated corpses. But for Ryza, the bloodshed represents a path of redemption for an upbringing he's just escaped.

His prowess with a rifle draws the interest of the Locusts, a clandestine faction within Revance's ranks. It turns out that not all aboard the fortress seek to stamp out the plague of molten flux, the mysterious liquid metal that fills the bodies of the dead and makes them walk again.

Some seek to profit.

The reanimated corpses —known as autominds— are used to control enormous contraptions of magnetically enchanted metal, forming the backbone of The Droughtland's factories. The only thing stopping the smelters from expanding their illicit industry is Revance.

The Locusts make Ryza an offer. Either help overthrow

Revance to do the smelter's bidding or reveal his father's legacy as the very thing Ryza now fights against.

The former is unthinkable. The latter means death.

Ryza resolves to infiltrate them and expose the mutiny, plunging him back into the murky underworld of the smelters, testing his convictions, and even leading him to the ancient origins of molten flux itself.

Released on 17/06/2023, MOLTEN FLUX is the first book of the Flux Catastrophe series. Drawing inspiration from both Mad Max: Fury Road and The Mortal Engines series, readers of fantasy and science fiction alike will find thrilling action and brutal battles in a world of sandstorms and scrap metal.

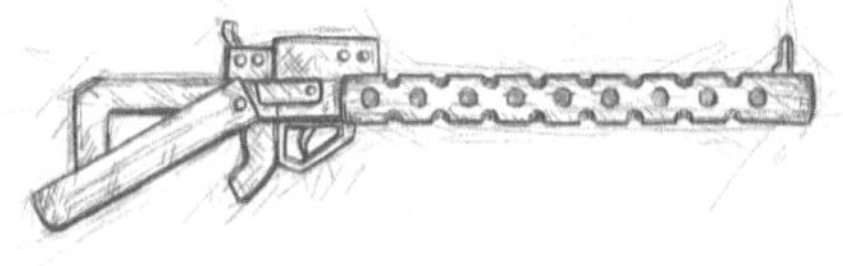

CANYON CAPTIVES

RYZA COULD TASTE SAND at one corner of his lips and blood at the other. He glanced at the man who'd just struck him. He was shirtless, scarred and covered in filth.

Typical smelter.

The man brandished his scrap metal club at Ryza, threatening another blow if he didn't get moving. In order to avoid being knocked senseless, he bitterly obeyed. Ryza's gift from the smelter was a set of box-like cuffs that bound his wrists, sharp wire biting into his skin. The blood running down his temple made his cropped hair redder than usual. The smelter that had cuffed him shouted something guttural and shoved Ryza into the line of similarly restrained men.

Walls of red rocks reached high on either side, the last signs of daylight brushing over the cliff's edge. The sky had been blue when their trade caravan entered the canyon, now it was a bruised purple. In hindsight, the decision to travel this route was extremely foolish.

They'd been halfway through when a single man holding a dagger stepped from the shadows and brought the whole procession to a grinding halt. Smelters had appeared in front and behind them, ten in total, all with makeshift weapons in one hand, a bag of cuffs in the other, and a hungry grin on their faces.

The line of docile merchants shambled forward and Ryza moved with them. Leaning to his right, he could see what was happening at the front. Each man's cuffs were being threaded with a long length of chain before the chain was passed to the next prisoner. Ryza looked down at his restraints.

It was a small square of thick metal with a slot on each side for wrists to be bound by thick wire. In the middle, a small hole had been drilled for a chain to be passed through. The damn thing was more rust that iron, but no matter how much Ryza struggled against it, he couldn't break free on his own.

The smelter with the chain slapped the man he was attending to on the back of the head, sending him stumbling into the group of the restrained traders, then beckoned to the next man.

The line shambled forwards. Ryza was now next to the caravan's carts. Three men with crowbars busted them open with glee and rummaged around, looting anything they perceived as valuable. Sacks of reels, bundled furs, glinting jewels, and most importantly, water.

Legend had it people once drank the precious stuff. Eons ago when it still rained in this desert land. But one day people just stopped needing to. It was all in the air. Now water was scarce, used only for the concoction of magical inks, inks that would be painted as runes onto the skin where their meaning could be cast as axioms into the world, axioms that could set him free.

He looked down at his wrists. One blocky green rune peeked out from under the restraints. This one could manipulate the magnetism of a piece of metal if he was touching it, enough to break him out of these damn cuffs. In his mind, he could picture the metal wires holding his wrists snapping like twine. But then what would he do? Get beaten to death by ten smelters, most likely, but at least he would die a free man. There was a small vial of green ink stashed in his underpants, but by the time he had painted another rune on his arm, his head would be inside out.

The line shuffled forward again. There were only three people in front of him. He needed a plan, fast. Unconsciously, he began chewing his top lip. He'd done this ever since he was small, it just seemed to help him think. Ryza could still remember when his father had taught him that some animals could be instantly calmed by holding their upper lip. Maybe he was right about that, but he'd also been wrong about a whole lot else.

The chainer pulled the next man into position. Two left until it was Ryza's turn. He glanced around quickly. There was no way he could outrun the smelters. He might be fast and lean, but they would catch up to him before he made it out of the canyon. No matter which direction he chose, there would be at least a mile until he hit open desert. That wasn't an option. The cliff walls would be working against him. But what if he could use them?

His train of thought was interrupted by a shout from the caravan's half-looted carts.

'Water!'

Whoops of delight echoed through the canyon and the smelters swarmed to it. The caravan had set out with an entire bucket of water, enough to trade for a town's worth of reels. Now it would just go to waste in the hands of these wretches. Ryza didn't care. They could have it. That bucket of water may have just bought him his escape. Three men ran past him from the front. Four men were already on the carts.

Ryza looked over his shoulder. Having run out of cuffs, the smelter that had all but concussed him was idly standing guard at the back of the halted convoy. There were now only three men he needed to get past. The chainer, the smelter corralling the chained merchants, and the man who had stopped the caravan in the first place, who was standing about twenty metres away and playing with his pathetically small dagger.

The chainer had paused for a moment in the commotion but was now turned back to the man in front of him. Ryza watched his every motion closely. First, the chainer placed his club down, leaning it against his leg as he fumbled the excessively long iron coil through the cuffs. Once that was done, the man in question received a quick tap from the club to move him along. The whole process took maybe a minute at best.

The man ahead of Ryza stepped forward and he followed. If he could pop the cuffs off fast enough, he could get to the club before the chainer could grab it, then he'd have to dart back to avoid being grabbed. The chainer would still have that length of chain to swing with, but that wasn't a match for the vicious looking weapon. The only problem would be that Ryza would have to fight the other man at the same time. Even if he could dispatch both, the rest of the smelters would be on him.

'Cuffs,' the chainer grunted at the man ahead, placing down his club and holding out his hand.

But the man hesitated. Ryza watched his shoulders tense. Maybe he was thinking of an escape, too. Ryza swore under his breath. It didn't matter if this man made it out or not, Ryza's plan was now ruined.

'Cuffs!' the chainer demanded.

'You can have 'em!' the man roared. He followed through with a vicious upper cut, aiming the edge of his cuffs at the chainer's chin.

But the chainer was quicker, deftly dodging the blow with a step back, scooping up his club as he went. One swing would have been enough to put the man in his place, but the chainer seemed to think a bit more discipline was needed. Each lumbering blow came crushing down on the man's skull, cracking into bone before squelching through brain, sending an explosive burst of blood and giblets in every direction.

By the time the man's lifeless corpse collapsed, both Ryza and the chainer were covered in blood. Ryza could feel the warmth of it soaking through his shirt. He could feel his breathing quicken. If that was the result of a failed plan, he might as well ask to be clubbed too.

The nearest smelter approached them, giving the body a light kick and grunting.

'Bit of a mess there,' he said to the chainer.

The chainer croaked with laughter. 'Yer' telling me! A bit o' flux ain't fixing that!' He turned to Ryza and offered him a toothless grin. 'Sorry 'bout the mess. Looks like we'll both be this filthy for a week.'

Ryza shuddered at the thought. Packed in a cage with the others while covered in a dead man's blood. He'd rather die. They'd kill him anyway once they were ready, only to pump his corpse full of molten flux and make it walk once more. It's how the bastards got the name "smelter" in the first place. Ryza shuddered again. The silvery substance was unnerving enough to look at in a glass vial. He couldn't imagine it coursing through his veins.

The chainer beckoned him forward, but Ryza hesitated. The chainer still hadn't put down his club. He glanced over at the other smelter. He was too close. Ryza could attack the chainer, but the other man would be on him before he was out of the cuffs.

The smelter moved closer, his shoulder almost bumping against Ryza's. 'Wouldn't be thinking of doing the same, now would you?'

Ryza resisted wincing as the man's breath engulfed his face, the scent of long rotted meat. 'I've got enough blood on me for the day,' Ryza said, struggling to keep his voice level.

The smelter and the chainer cackled, throwing their heads back. Ryza glanced over his shoulder while they were distracted. None of the other smelters had noticed the commotion. They were still too busy with the looted cart.

The chainer moved closer, his left shoulder just next to Ryza's right.

'You're a funny one, I always like that in an automind,' the chainer said. 'Hope the flux can bring that back with ya.'

The chainer placed his club down, resting it against his right knee and Ryza swore inwardly. The chainer and the smelter were facing each other in front of him, they'd have him by the neck before he could dive for the weapon. Ryza glanced at the smelter on his left. He was holding his own club loosely in his right hand. If he could just get to it first.

Ryza began concentrating on the rune inked into his left wrist, imagining it sliding into his clenched fist. Almost hearing the loud *ping* the cuffs would make as the wire snapped out with deadly force. Ryza's eyes widened.

That was it!

'Now let's not have any more trouble here. Let's see them cuffs.'

'Of course,' Ryza said with a grin.

He whipped them up to neck level and clamped his eyes shut, forcing the rune in his hand to burn white-hot.

Feel the metal.

Become the metal.

Revel in it.

His father's words ran through his head as an ethereal feeling flowed into the wire, as if it were an extension of his hands. It was his. His to control.

The wire whipped through the air and Ryza's fists flew apart, bursting out of the cuffs and slamming into the faces of the men on either side. It would have been a stunning blow to each of them, enough to send them staggering back, roaring in pain.

But when Ryza opened his eyes, it was to a gurgling silence. His fists were drenched in blood. On either side of him, the men were clutching at their throats, metal wire embedded in each of their necks. Ryza couldn't believe his luck.

That's what they get for giving a Kretatic enough metal.

The club was in Ryza's hands before the chainer's body hit the ground and he sprinted at the smelter still playing with his dagger. They only looked up when Ryza was two paces away, but it was far too late for him.

Ryza made a wide, one-handed swing with the club that would devastate whatever it hit. The blow landed right in the centre of the man's face, the weighty club head caving his skull in with ease. They collapsed into the dust, but Ryza had already sprinted on.

He was scanning the cliff walls as he fled, looking for that one bit of extra rocky surface that he could scramble up. As a child, he'd climbed and subsequently fallen off enough things that he considered himself as nimble on a wall as he was on the ground. He only had to hope that the smelters weren't similarly gifted. And that they didn't find the crates of pristine rifles hidden in the rear carts.

A shout of alarm filled the canyon behind him. The smelters had caught on. But it didn't matter, Ryza was already a good two hundred metres away from them and he'd found exactly what he was looking for. On one side the cliff creased in on itself, just enough to form a narrow rocky shaft that went all the way to the top.

Ryza began climbing it with ease, finding handholds and footholds without even looking. It was only when he was halfway up that he looked down and realised just how much blood was on his hands. At least it wasn't his.

Not yet.

Down below, the remaining smelters had caught up to him. Some of what they were shouting at him might have been words, but Ryza wasn't focused on them. If he turned back to yell at them, if he got cocky, he might as well just let go and fall to his death. However, his focus shook as a loud clang came from somewhere below.

One of the smelters hurled a freshly pillaged rifle at him, the improvised javelin only making it halfway up the cliff before clattering back down harmlessly. The idea caught on and soon all seven of them were hurling their own clubs and machetes at Ryza, none of them coming nearly high enough to hit him. He allowed himself a smirk, but it was wiped off his face when a dagger bounced off the piece of rock he was about to put his hand on. He scrambled higher, a little faster than he was comfortable with, but soon he was clambering over the edge of the cliff.

There was no chance of the smelters following and by the time they reached the top, Ryza would be long gone. He looked to his right at the now unattended caravan. The few men that hadn't been cuffed were now attempting to unchain the rest.

Now they work together.

Ryza hadn't heard a single friendly word for the two weeks since the caravan had left Breggesa. Every single person down there had been out to make their own fortune. He hadn't even learnt any of their names because of how little they spoke about anything that wasn't reels.

At least they weren't trading in molten flux.

They could fend for themselves now. They would probably be recaptured once the remaining smelters realised what was going on. But Ryza was free. All he had to do was find the next trading post and hitch a ride.

Ryza turned around, ready to set off west, but was met with a sight that made his jaw drop. There was no horizon. Instead, all he could see was a tumultuous wall of sand, as high as the sky itself. It was rapidly bearing down on him, sucking up the dunes as fuel. Ryza could feel the oncoming gusts on his tongue. This one would be vicious, more vicious than the smelters down below. Suddenly, the canyon was looking mighty inviting.

Ryza swore to himself. He needed shelter. A cave would be perfect, but as he scanned the land, the only thing he saw was a rocky outcrop. He looked back up at the sandstorm. It seemed to have doubled in size in the time he hadn't been watching it. Enormous dark shapes were shifting in the belly of the thrashing haze.

Ryza began sprinting again, almost losing control of his legs as he belted down the sandy slope for the rocks. Before, it had been a simple race against the wits of some smelters, but now he was competing with the fury of the desert itself. If he hadn't secreted among those rocks by the time the storm hit, he'd be flung sky high by the howling wind. Ryza could feel it pushing against him, slowing his stride as the dunes began to shift under his feet.

He was almost there, but the sandstorm was closer. The rocks disappeared in an instant, but Ryza kept running. The wall of dust was upon him now, stretching over him like a monster's jaws, tendrils of sand reaching out for him.

Ryza burst into it.

He felt his feet leave the ground.

For more bonuses just like this one, make sure to sign up to my mailing list, where I send through monthly updates on writing progress, deleted scenes, short stories and exclusive offers from myself and other awesome independent authors.

Just go to https://jonathanweiss.com.au/contact and enter your details.